TIGER
DAYS

A book of feelings

Written by M.H. Clark
Illustrated by Anna Hurley

On TIGER DAYS I want to climb.

I'M WILD AND I'M FIERCE.

I pace around and POUNCE and ROAR,

that's just what tiger days are for.

On SNAIL DAYS I go SLOWLY
in everything I do.

AND I MIGHT TAKE A LITTLE WHILE,

when I'm a snail that's just my style.

On RABBIT DAYS I'm wide awake.
I RUN AND SKIP AND JUMP.

And when I start to HOP and HOP,
it feels like I might never stop!

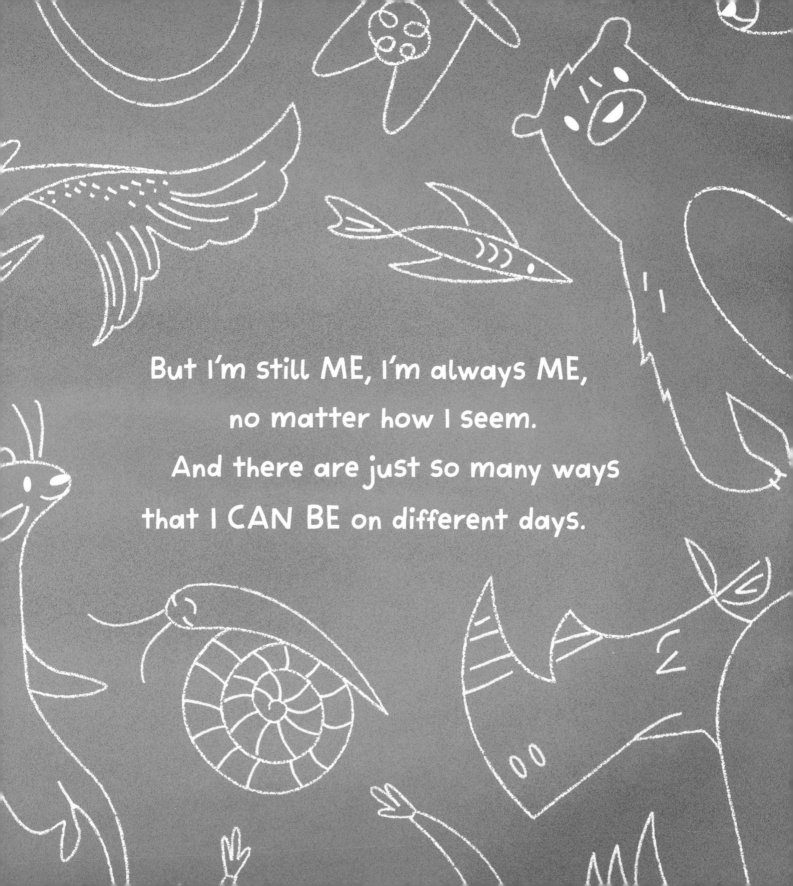

But I'm still ME, I'm always ME,
no matter how I seem.
And there are just so many ways
that I CAN BE on different days.

On TURTLE DAYS, I'm quiet.
On turtle days, I'M SHY.
I don't have much I want to say,
I'D RATHER HIDE MY FACE AWAY.

On BEAR DAYS I go lumbering,

I FEEL SO BIG AND STRONG.

No matter what the day might bring,

I think I COULD DO ANYTHING.

On FISH DAYS I feel watery,
SO SAD AND FULL OF TEARS.

And even if I don't know why,
I need to JUST SIT STILL and CRY.

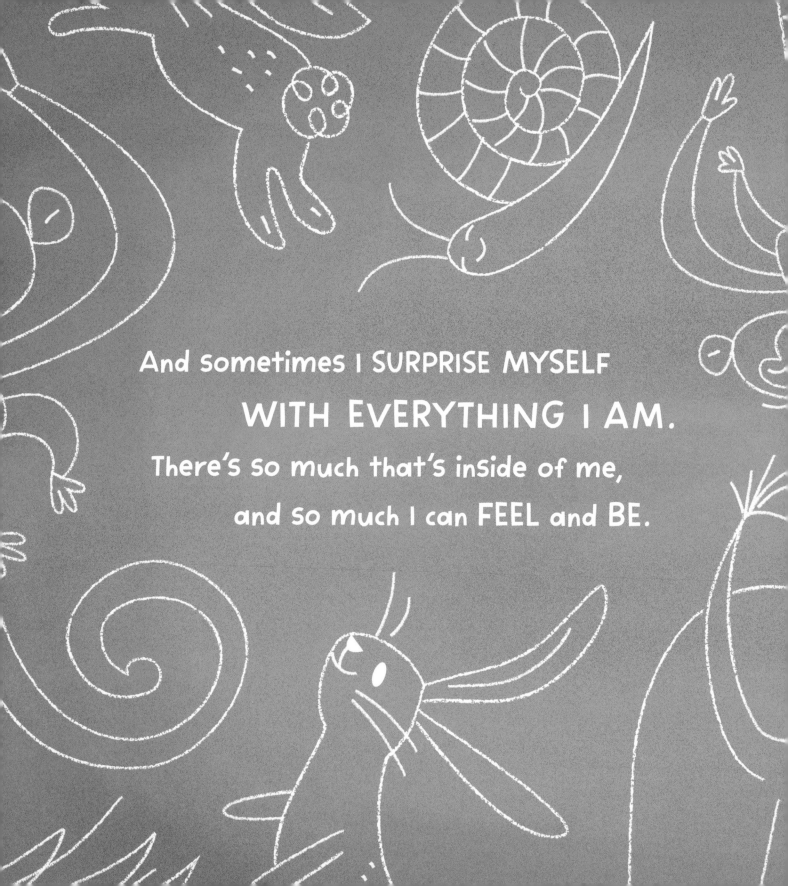

And sometimes I SURPRISE MYSELF
WITH EVERYTHING I AM.
There's so much that's inside of me,
and so much I can FEEL and BE.

On MONKEY DAYS I'm SILLY
and I'm ready for some FUN.

I WANT TO LAUGH AND SWING AND PLAY
and be around my friends all day.

On BULL DAYS I'm so full of RAGE,
I stomp around the room.

I shake my head and YELL and SHOUT
AND LET MY ANGRY FEELINGS OUT.

On RHINO DAYS I'm STUBBORN.

DON'T TELL ME WHAT TO DO!

No matter what you think or say,

I want to do it all MY WAY.

Some days I feel so WILD and BRAVE
and some days I feel small.
There are so MANY WAYS to be
when you're as big inside as ME.

On PARROT DAYS I'm loud and bright,
I have so much to say.

I TALK A LOT AND LAUGH AND SING,

I want to tell you EVERYTHING.

On OTTER DAYS I hug you LOTS
and hold your hand in mine.
I want some extra CUDDLES too,
I LOVE TO BE RIGHT NEXT TO YOU.

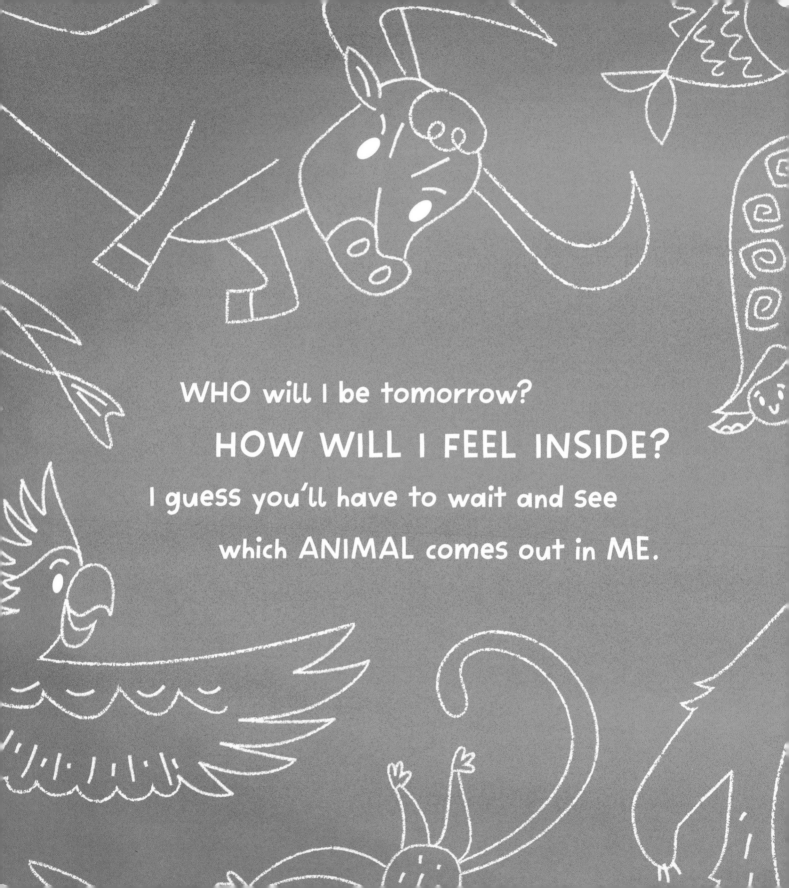

WHO will I be tomorrow?
HOW WILL I FEEL INSIDE?
I guess you'll have to wait and see
which ANIMAL comes out in ME.

COMPENDIUM®
live inspired

Written by: M.H. Clark

Illustrated by: Anna Hurley

Edited by: Ruth Austin

Designed and Art Directed by: Sarah Forster

Library of Congress Control Number: 2018941325 | ISBN: 978-1-946873-41-5

3rd printing. Printed in China with soy inks on FSC®-Mix certified paper. A092110003

Create meaningful moments with gifts that inspire.

CONNECT WITH US
live-inspired.com | sayhello@compendiuminc.com

   @compendiumliveinspired
#compendiumliveinspired